The Case Of The
Christmas
CAPER™

A novelization by Jean Waricha

WILL SOLVE ANY CRIME • BY DINNER TIME™

DUALSTAR PUBLICATIONS   PARACHUTE PRESS, INC.

SCHOLASTIC INC.

New York   Toronto   London   Auckland   Sydney

DUALSTAR PUBLICATIONS ™ PARACHUTE PRESS, INC.

Dualstar Publications
c/o 10100 Santa Monica Blvd.
Suite 2200
Los Angeles, CA 90067

Parachute Press, Inc.
156 Fifth Avenue
Suite 325
New York, NY 10010

Published by Scholastic Inc.

Copyright © 1996 Dualstar Entertainment Group, Inc. All rights reserved.
All photography copyright © 1996 Dualstar Entertainment Group, Inc.
All rights reserved.

The Adventures of Mary-Kate & Ashley, Mary-Kate + Ashley's Fun Club, Clue and all
logos, character names, and other distinctive likenesses thereof are the trademarks of
Dualstar Entertainment Group, Inc. All rights reserved.

With special thanks to Robert Thorne and Harold Weitzberg.

If you purchased this book without a cover, you should be aware that this book is
stolen property. It was reported as "unsold and destroyed" to the publisher, and
neither the author nor the publisher has received payment for this "stripped book."

No part of this publication may be reproduced in whole or in part, or stored in a
retrieval system, or transmitted in any form or by any means, electronic, mechanical,
photocopying, recording, or otherwise, without written permission of the publisher.

Printed in the U.S.A.
December 1996
ISBN: 0-590-88009-8
B C D E F G H I J

Ready for Adventure?

It was the best of times. It was the worst of times. Actually it was bedtime when our great-grandmother would read us stories of mystery and suspense. It was then that we decided to be detectives.

The story you are about to read is one of the cases from the files of the Olsen and Olsen Mystery Agency. We call it *The Case Of The Christmas Caper.*

Ashley and I had never heard of E.L.F. Airlines before we got a call for help from Nick, Rick, and Slick. Their airplane, the *Spirit of Christmas*, was missing. And it had to make a very important delivery. If Ashley and I didn't find their plane, kids all over the world would have a very un-merry Christmas!

Suddenly, we were hot on the trail of the thief who stole the *Spirit of Christmas*. We had to stop him from being naughty, and make sure that this Christmas was extra nice. Because, no matter what, we always live up to our motto: Will Solve Any Crime By Dinner Time!

Chapter 1

"Ashley," I cried, "who's been eating the Christmas cookies? We're not supposed to eat them until tomorrow!"

"Don't look at me. I didn't eat them," Ashley said. "I'm too busy wrapping these Christmas presents."

Ashley was surrounded by a stack of boxes. There were presents for our mom and dad, our little sister, Lizzie, our big brother, Trent, and Clue, our brown-and-white basset hound.

I lifted a half-eaten Christmas cookie. "Well, if you didn't eat them," I said, "and I didn't eat them—"

"Then it looks like we've got a mystery on our hands," Ashley said.

My name is Mary-Kate Olsen. My twin sister, Ashley, and I are the Trenchcoat Twins. We solve crimes. We love mysteries! We're detectives!

Right now we were in the office of the Olsen and Olsen Mystery Agency. It's in the attic of our house. We have lots of equipment here to help us solve crimes, including our magnifying glasses.

Ashley grabbed her magnifying glass and held it over the chewed-up cookie. "Wait a minute," she said. "I recognize these teeth marks."

She pointed at Clue. Clue is more than our pet. She's also our silent partner. She helps us solve crimes. Her nose is a super-duper snooper—perfect for sniffing out clues.

"Clue, are you using your super-power nose to sniff out some fresh-baked Christmas cookies?" Ashley asked.

We both rushed over to the chair where Clue was lying down. Ashley lifted Clue's front paws. Underneath them lay a whole pile of cookies.

"Another mystery solved," Ashley said. "But that one was way too easy," she added.

"Yeah," I said. "The really tough mystery is figuring out how we'll ever be ready for Christmas tomorrow! We have cards to write, presents to wrap, stockings to stuff, and the tree to trim."

"And thanks to Clue, we have more cookies to bake," Ashley added. "Well, let's just take one thing at a time," she said.

Ashley is always cool, calm, and collected. Not like me. In fact, sometimes it's hard to believe that we're twins. We're both nine years old. We both have strawberry blond hair and big blue eyes. We look alike. But we sure don't act alike. Or think alike!

Ashley likes to take her time with everything, especially when we're trying to solve a case. Not me. I like to jump right in.

"Let's trim the tree first," I said to Ashley.

"That's our most important job."

Ashley nodded. This Christmas is the first time that our parents let us have our own tree to decorate. Mom lent us some of her special glass ornaments. Dad found a big silver foil star to place on top. And Great-grandma Olive sent us strings of Christmas lights.

We went to work.

"It looks fantastic," I said when we were finished.

Our desk phones rang, and we ran to answer them. We each have our own phone. Mine is pink and Ashley's is blue.

"Olsen and Olsen Mystery Agency," we said at the same time.

"Will solve any crime…" I began.

"By dinner time!" Ashley finished.

"Help," a squeaky voice answered. "I'm Nick, here with Rick and Slick. We're from E.L.F. Airlines. That stands for Extremely Long Flights. And we've got an extremely big problem. We lost the *Spirit of Christmas*!"

"Try singing a few Christmas carols," Ashley said.

"Great idea," I added. "Singing gives me lots of Christmas spirit!" We began to sing. "Jingle bells…jingle bells…jingle all the—"

"No, no…you don't understand," Nick shouted. "The *Spirit of Christmas* is the name of our airplane," he explained.

"Our very important airplane," Rick added. "And it's missing."

"How did you lose an airplane?" I asked.

"We don't know! That's the mystery," Nick answered. "Our plane has to make very special deliveries all over the world," he added. "And they have to be made by tomorrow morning—or our customers will be *very* unhappy."

"But tomorrow is Christmas day," I told him.

"Exactly!" Nick, Rick, and Slick yelled.

I turned to Ashley. "We can't let *anyone*

be unhappy on Christmas morning," I said.

"You're right," she said.

We both spoke into the phone. "Say no more. We're on our way!"

Nick, Rick, and Slick gave us the address for E.L.F. Airlines. It was 1225 North Pole Drive.

"Isn't the North Pole where Santa Claus lives?" Ashley asked.

"Yes. And it's also where he and his helpers make all the toys," I added.

"But *that* North Pole is at the top of the world. It's cold and snowy there all year round," Ashley said. "E.L.F. Airlines is right here in warm, sunny California."

Ashley reached into the desk drawer and pulled out a map. She spread it across the desk and checked it out. "Here it is!" she exclaimed, pointing to a spot on the map. "We're not going to the *real* North Pole. 1225 North Pole Drive is only a bike ride away."

I looked at the clock. It was almost noon. "We'd better hurry," I told Ashley. "If we don't leave now, we'll never find the *Spirit of Christmas* before Christmas morning."

I packed up my notebook and my detective manual. Ashley and I never forget our detective manuals. They were gifts from Great-grandma Olive. Any time we're stumped, we check the manual for ideas.

Ashley packed our magnifying glasses and our fingerprinting kit. "Let's go!" she said.

The door to the attic swung open. Trent burst into the room.

Trent is eleven and a total pain. He was huffing and puffing and all out of breath.

"Boy, those stairs are tough," Trent said. "Especially when you're carrying a really heavy box."

Trent held a big square box wrapped in colorful holiday paper. A shiny red bow was perched on top.

"This weighs a ton. That means there's

something good inside!" Trent told us.

"We know what it is," I said. "Mom and Dad are giving us laptop computers for Christmas. You know, the kind of computers that you can carry with you."

"And they said we don't have to wait to open them," Ashley said.

"Great," Trent said. "I lugged the box upstairs, so I get to open it!"

Trent began to tear at the wrapping paper.

"Wait, Trent!" Ashley shrieked. "It's our present, so *we* should open it." She jumped at the box.

"Watch it!" Trent yelled. He lost his balance. The package dropped out of his hands. Trent fell backward—right into our Christmas tree.

The tree wobbled and swayed.

Craaash! Craaack!

Our beautiful tree smashed onto the floor. The lights flickered out. Some of Mom's glass ornaments shattered. Dad's silver foil star flew off, hit the floor, and crumpled.

"Oh, no!" Ashley exclaimed. "Our tree is ruined!"

Ashley and I stared at the mess. The tree had knocked over our big supply shelf. Books, pencils, paper clips, and spare notebooks lay scattered over the floor, mixed with pieces of broken glass.

"What a mess," I sighed. "Mom and Dad will never let us have our own tree again!"

Our parents raced into the room. "What was that horrible noise?" Mom asked. She spotted the fallen tree and gasped.

"Are you kids all right?" she asked.

We all nodded yes.

Mom frowned. "I thought you were more responsible than this," she scolded. "I guess I was wrong."

"Clean up this mess before dinner time," Dad told Ashley and me.

Our parents left the room.

I glared at Trent. "This is your fault," I

said. "You knocked over the tree."

Ashley and I pushed the tree to one side. Underneath was the big box. Its sides had split open. Our brand-new laptop computers lay on the floor.

"Hey—these computers are just what we need now," I said. "They can help us find the *Spirit of Christmas*!"

Ashley and I quickly packed the computers into our backpacks. "Let's go," I said. We passed Trent and headed for the door.

"Wait!" Ashley exclaimed. "We forgot to clean up this mess."

"But we have to get to E.L.F. Airlines!" I told her.

"You're right," Ashley agreed. "We'll clean up *after* dinner." She headed for the door.

"You'd better do it now," Trent warned us.

"We'll do it later," I told him. "We have an important case to solve."

We raced down the stairs and out of the house. Our bikes were waiting in the driveway. So was Clue.

"Good girl, Clue!" I patted her head. "I hope that super-duper snooper of yours can help us sniff out a missing airplane!"

Chapter 3

"E.L.F. sure is a small airline," Ashley said.

We stopped our bikes in front of a flashing red sign that spelled out "Extremely Long Flights." In front of us was the airport's headquarters. Behind the headquarters was the runway where the planes landed. The initials E.L.F. were painted at the end of the runway. Off to the left side was the airplane hangar.

A hangar is like a garage where planes park. The hangar doors were wide open. And the hangar was empty.

"Where are Nick, Slick, and Rick?" Ashley asked.

"I don't know," I answered.

I patted Clue on the head. "Sniff around, Clue. See if you can find three guys who look like a Nick, a Slick, and a Rick," I said.

Clue sniffed the air. She ran off. A moment later we heard her bark.

"There they are!" Ashley pointed down the runway. "Clue found them!"

Nick, Slick, and Rick were only about three feet tall. They were grown-ups, but they were no taller than us.

They wore bright blue overalls with their names spelled out on the pockets. They had chubby bodies and red faces. They each had a mop of curly red hair. And Nick had a curly red beard.

"Merry, merry, merry Christmas," they sang out, as they ran up to us.

Nick stepped forward. He seemed to be their leader. "You must be Mary-Kate and Ashley," Nick said. "We're glad to see you!"

"Uh—and we're glad to see *you*," I said.

"But you also seem *surprised* to see us," Nick added.

"Happens every time," Rick said.

"Never fails," Slick added. "People never get used to it."

"Get used to what?" I asked them.

"Why, our height, of course," Nick answered. "People stare at us because we're so small. Is that what surprised you?"

"Nooooo...," Ashley and I both began to say. Nick, Rick, and Slick raised their bushy red eyebrows as if they didn't believe us.

"Well, yessss...," we said instead.

"Don't worry. We don't mind being small," Slick told us.

"Not at all," Rick agreed. "Where we come from, *everybody* is small."

"You can call us 'little people.' Little people with a great big job and one big mystery," Nick added.

"So let's get started!" Ashley exclaimed.

I whipped out my notebook. "We need to know everything about E.L.F. Airlines and how you lost the *Spirit of Christmas*," I said.

"We'd better go inside," Nick said.

We hurried inside the hangar with Nick, Slick, and Rick. Clue ran after us, staying close to Nick.

"Clue really seems to like Nick," I said. "I wonder why?"

Ashley shrugged. Nick led us into a huge room with a very high ceiling.

"Wow!" Ashley shouted. "Look at the blinking lights. They're all red and green."

"This is our control room," Nick told us.

We stared at rows and rows of computers and two computer printers. Maps and charts covered the walls. Hundreds of electrical wires ran across the floor. One computer was so big, it took up a whole wall.

"This is where it all happens," Nick announced. "These computers, charts, and maps help us to run E.L.F."

"They keep track of the planes. And they tell us which way the planes should fly," Rick added.

"Yup. Yup. You don't want planes to

crash into each other," Slick put in.

"We can track planes all over the world," Nick told us. "Why, we can track five hundred planes at once!"

Ashley and I looked at each other in surprise. "But you have only one plane," Ashley said.

"And didn't you *lose* it?" I asked.

Nick's face turned red. "Yes," he said. "But there's a reason. We used our newest computer to track the *Spirit of Christmas*!"

Nick pointed to the giant computer. The one that covered the entire wall. "We used that one. The really BIG computer."

Nick's eyes lit up with pride. "It's a one-of-a-kind, one hundred percent foolproof, flood-proof, earthquake-proof system," Nick explained.

Hmmm.

I scribbled some notes. PROBLEM: The *Spirit of Christmas* is missing. CLUES: The really BIG computer lost track of it. WHEN: ?

21

I turned to Nick. "When *exactly* did you lose the *Spirit of Christmas*?" I asked.

Nick looked at his watch. "About an hour ago. Right, Rick?"

"Right," Rick answered. "Nick and I were tracking the plane with our computers."

"And I was making popcorn," Slick added.

"The plane took off from Mistletoe Mountain," Nick explained. "It was time to use the BIG computer to bring her in for a landing. But the BIG computer didn't work!"

"And we haven't a clue why," Rick said.

"Well, do you know how to use the really BIG computer?" I asked.

Nick lowered his head. "Uh...not yet! We just got it yesterday," he added.

"Maybe we should call Mom and Dad and ask them," I told Ashley.

Our parents are computer experts. That's their job. They know everything there is to know about all sorts of computers.

Ashley reached for her magnifying glass.

"Let's search for some clues first," she suggested.

Ashley knelt down on the floor and crawled behind the BIG computer. "I just found out what the problem is," she called out. "And I know we can fix it!"

Ashley crawled out from behind the computer. In her hand she held the plug of an electrical cord. "The computer wasn't plugged in!" she exclaimed.

"Oops," Slick said. His face turned almost as red as his hair. "I unplugged that when I used the popcorn popper."

Nick and Rick stared at him in surprise.

"Well, at least the mystery is solved," I said.

Ashley plugged the cord into the socket in the wall. We heard a loud whirring sound. The really BIG computer lit up.

"Hooray!" Nick shouted. "It's working!"

"You've done it!" Rick yelled.

Nick, Rick, and Slick hugged each other.

"Merry, merry, merry Christmas!" they all cried.

"Woof! Woof!" Clue barked. Nick patted her on the head.

A loud voice suddenly boomed into the room. "Ho! Ho! Ho!"

"Hey—that sounds like…" I began.

"Nah, couldn't be," Ashley said.

"But think about it," I went on. "It's almost Christmas Eve. The *Spirit of Christmas* has to make very important deliveries all over the world. What if the pilot really is—"

At that moment a picture flashed onto the huge computer monitor.

A plump, cheery man sat in the cockpit of an airplane. A man with white hair sticking out of a red leather flight helmet. A man with a long white beard that flowed over his enormous belly.

"Woof!" Clue barked in excitement. She ran back and forth in front of the screen.

Ashley grabbed my arm. "You're right!

That looks just like Sant—"

Nick lifted his finger to his lips. "Shhh," he whispered. "Let's just keep this our little secret!"

"But now you know why it's so important to land the plane," Rick added. "The *Spirit of Christmas* has to stop here at E.L.F. to pick up its special delivery and then continue on its way."

"We get it," I told Nick and his friends. "And don't worry—your secret is safe with us. We promise."

We all turned to the big monitor.

"Hello, E.L.F. Central!" the white-bearded pilot shouted. His bright eyes sparkled. "This is S.C. in the *Spirit of Christmas* calling! Ho, ho, ho! Over."

Nick grabbed a microphone and shouted back. "Hello, S.C. We had a tiny problem," Nick told him. He glared at Slick. "But thanks to Olsen and Olsen, we're up and running now," Nick finished.

"That's what I wanted to hear!" S.C. exclaimed. "Now we'll make our deliveries by Christmas morning!" He winked. "And I'll get to eat all those delicious cookies our customers will leave for me."

"Where are you now?" Nick asked.

"I'm somewhere in the mountains," S.C. told him. "And I need directions out of here."

Slick grabbed the microphone from Nick. "No problem, S.C. The BIG computer will tell you where to go! This will be a piece of cake—sugar-frosted Christmas cake!"

S.C. began to laugh. His big belly jiggled up and down.

"Okay," he shouted. "The computer is sending directions right now. I should touch down in about ten minutes, and—"

The big monitor made a loud buzzing noise. The sound of static filled the air. The TV screen went blank. S.C. was gone. And so was the *Spirit of Christmas*!

"What happened now?" Nick shouted.

"Where did he go?" Slick yelled.

A loud popping sound came from the BIG computer.

"What was that?" Rick shrieked.

Then everything started to happen at once. The BIG computer sparked and sputtered—and then it went dead.

The red and green lights flickered and went out.

The small computer screens popped and crackled and flashed off.

The control room was completely dark.

Nick rushed to a cabinet and grabbed flashlights. He tossed them to all of us. Rick shone his on the computer keyboards. Slick tried turning on as many switches as he could find. Nothing worked.

"We lost him!" Rick shouted in horror. "We lost the *Spirit of Christmas* again!"

Ka-blooom!

Sparks flew out of the BIG computer.

"Look! What does that mean?" I shouted. I pointed to the big screen where we had just been watching S.C.

On the screen two words appeared in giant, bold letters:

BAH, HUMBUG!

Chapter 5

"Bah, humbug?" Ashley read the words. "I never heard *that* expression before. Have you?" she asked me.

"Nope. I don't know what it means," I told her. "But I know one thing for sure."

"What's that?" Ashley asked.

"Olsen and Olsen are back on the case," I said.

"Do you think we're dealing with a tracker?" Slick asked.

"I think you mean a 'hacker,'" Ashley told him. "A computer hacker is someone who breaks into a computer and scrambles the information inside," she explained.

"No way anyone could break inside *this* computer," Rick told us. "It's locked shut."

"Yup, it is. And there are no doors to go through either," Slick added.

Ashley and I shook our heads and laughed.

"That's not what Ashley means," I said. "There's no one inside the computer!"

"No. I mean that someone is using *their* computer to control *your* computer," Ashley added. "They found a way to make it shut down."

"How did they do that?" Slick asked.

"They probably got hold of your secret code," I told him. "The code that lets you talk to your computer."

"What is your secret code?" I asked.

"Ho! Ho! Ho!" Nick laughed loudly.

I frowned. "This is no time for jokes," I said. "Be serious."

"I *am* being serious," Nick said. "*Ho! Ho! Ho!* is our secret code."

"Oh. Well, then, now we just need to find out who the hacker is," I said.

31

"And fast!" Ashley added. "And I know how to do it, too."

Ashley unpacked her new laptop computer. "Let's plug this into the BIG computer," she said.

"Let's start by typing in the secret code," I told her.

Ashley typed "Ho! Ho! Ho!" on her laptop.

The lights flashed on the BIG computer.

"You did it, Ashley! You got into the computer," I shouted.

Nick, Rick, and Slick cheered. Clue barked and wagged her tail.

"Yeah, but I don't know what I'm looking for. What information is stored in this computer?" Ashley asked Nick.

"A list of the places where we make deliveries on Christmas Eve," Nick told her.

"Hey, you can't tell them about that," Rick whispered to Nick. "S.C. told us to keep those lists a secret!"

"We *have* to tell," Nick whispered back.

"How else can they help us?"

Ashley and I exchanged a knowing look.

"Uh, Nick—do the lists have something to do with who's been naughty and who's been nice?" I asked.

Nick, Rick, and Slick stared at me in surprise. "How did you know that?" Nick asked.

"Just a lucky guess," I said.

"Don't tell anyone," Nick begged us. "No one is supposed to know where we keep our 'Naughty' and 'Nice' lists."

"It may be too late for that," Ashley pointed out. She typed some commands into her laptop.

"I found the file where the lists are stored," she announced.

"Are they okay?" Nick asked.

"Let's print them and find out," I said. Ashley pushed a button. We heard a couple of loud clicks.

"They're printing!" Nick announced. He ran over to the two printers. I saw that one printer was labeled "Nice." The other printer was labeled "Naughty."

The printers whirred and clicked. Sheets of paper flew out of the "Naughty" printer.

Nick grabbed the papers and quickly read through them. His cheerful red face turned pale. The twinkle went out of his eyes.

"Oh, no! This can't be!" he said. "Something is terribly wrong!"

Chapter 6

"What is it?" I asked Nick. "What's wrong?"

"See for yourselves," Nick said. He pointed at the "Naughty" printer. "I've never seen so many names on the 'Naughty' list," he said.

"Looks like every kid in the world is on it," Rick added.

"Let me see that list," I said. Ashley and I read through it.

"Wait a minute!" Ashley exclaimed. "Here's our sister, Lizzie...and here's Trent...and here's...us!"

Hmmm.

"Lizzie wasn't really naughty this year," Ashley said. "And Trent...well, maybe Trent *was* naughty," she added. "He did knock over our Christmas tree."

"But *we* haven't been naughty!" I said.

"Well, we *are* supposed to be cleaning our office right now," Ashley pointed out.

Nick tapped me on the shoulder. "Excuse me," he said. "But I think you need to see who's on the 'Nice' list."

"You're right," I said. Rick handed me the "Nice" list.

I gasped. "There's only one name here!"

Ashley grabbed the paper. She read the name out loud. "Ebenezer Scrooge."

"Do you think he's the hacker?" Nick asked.

"Could be," I answered. I flipped open my detective's notebook and wrote, SUSPECT: Ebenezer Scrooge.

"Wait a minute," Ashley said. "Let's be logical. Ebenezer Scrooge is a really weird name. So maybe the hacker made it up. He probably wouldn't use his real name anyway," she added.

"He wouldn't?" Slick asked.

"No. Using his real name would make him *too* easy to find," Ashley said. She shook her head. "That would be dumb. And we're dealing with one smart hacker," she added.

"Ashley's right," I said. "He *is* smart. First he figured out how to break into the really BIG computer to keep you from finding Santa and the *Spirit of Christmas*. And then he changed the 'Naughty' and 'Nice' lists," I finished.

"So we've got to be even smarter than he is to catch him," I said. "Now, what would Great-grandma Olive do in a case like this?"

"That's easy," Ashley replied. "She'd find out everything she could about our suspect."

"Wait a minute," Nick said. "I just remembered something. Ebenezer Scrooge is a name from a story. A famous Christmas story!"

"That makes sense," Ashley said. "Because our hacker is trying to ruin Christmas!"

Ashley quickly punched commands into her laptop.

"Now what are you doing?" Nick asked her. He, Rick, and Slick crowded close to Ashley. They stared at her laptop.

"I'm hooking up with the public library's computer information service," Ashley replied. "It tells about all kinds of stories."

Information flashed onto Ashley's computer screen. She read out loud.

"It says here that Ebenezer Scrooge is the main person in a famous story called 'A Christmas Carol,' by Charles Dickens," Ashley said. "Ebenezer Scrooge hated Christmas."

Ashley glanced up. "And guess what Scrooge used as his favorite expression?" she asked. "'Bah, humbug!'"

"Just like our hacker!" Nick exclaimed.

Slick stared at the name on the screen. "Ebenezer Scrooge," he said. "Yup, it's a funny name. It sounds like Ben E. Scrooge.

Or even Knees 'R' Scrooge." Slick giggled. "Or you could change the letters around and spell even funnier names," he added.

"That's it!" I shouted. "Slick, you're a genius!"

Slick beamed with pride. "What did I do?" he asked.

"You gave me our best clue yet," I said. "The letters in Ebenezer Scrooge *could* spell another name—the hacker's *real* name! It's a kind of code. Now all we have to do is crack the code," I explained.

Yes! Ashley and I slapped a high five.

"Let's start by typing the name Ebenezer Scrooge into our computer," Ashley said. "Then we'll tell the computer to switch the letters around until they spell a new name."

Ashley typed. Strange combinations of letters began flashing onto the screen. Suddenly the computer stopped.

"Look!" Nick exclaimed. "A name is on the screen!"

I read the name. "Roger E. Bencozees."

"We've got to find out if he's a real person. Let's check the telephone directory," Ashley told me.

I typed more commands into my laptop. "Here it is," I said. "Roger E. Bencozees the Third lives at 199 Highbrow Lane. Let's go!"

Ashley and I packed up our computers and our magnifying glasses. I shoved the stack of "Naughty" lists into my backpack.

"How long will it take to get there?" I asked Slick.

Slick scratched his beard. "It depends," he said. "Were you going to ride your bikes?"

"How else would we get there?" Ashley asked.

"I think there's another way," Slick said. "And it's a whole lot faster."

We're Mary-Kate and Ashley—the Trenchcoat
Twins. It was almost Christmas when we got a call
for help. Oh, no! Someone was in trouble on
Christmas Eve!

Nick, Rick, and Slick from E.L.F. Airlines needed us!
Someone had broken their computer. And they had
lost track of a plane with a very important delivery
to make before Christmas morning!

We jumped on our bikes and sped to E.L.F. Nick, Rick, and Slick were grownups, but they were small like us—with one *big* mystery to solve.

We had only ten hours to fix the computer, find the plane, help it land at E.L.F., load its special cargo—*and* make the delivery! We had no time to waste!

Problem solved! "Your computer isn't plugged in!" Ashley told Rick, Nick, and Slick. We plugged it in and waited to see what would happen next.

A picture of a plane flashed on the computer screen—and *Santa* was flying it! "Bring me in," Santa cried.

Suddenly the screen went black. The words BAH HUMBUG appeared. Now someone was trying to break into the computer system. But why?

The printers shot out lists of who had been naughty and nice. There was only one name on the Nice list—*Ebenezer Scrooge*. He was our suspect!

The name sounded like a scrambled code name to me. With my trusty laptop, I cracked the code! The suspect's real name was Roger E. Bencozees. And we knew just where to find him!

We all piled into Slick's car to pay Roger a visit.

He was just a 12-year-old boy! And he was trying to get all Santa's Christmas presents for himself!

We taught Roger that Christmas is a time to share. He felt bad for being greedy.

Ashley and I packed our bags. Our work was done.

Santa landed safely at E.L.F. Airlines and thanked us for saving Christmas for kids everywhere.

Faster than you can say Merry Christmas, Nick, Rick, and Slick changed into red and green outfits. Wow! Now we knew who they really were! Do you?

Chapter 7

"Wow!" My mouth dropped open in amazement. So did Ashley's.

"Cool wheels!" Ashley shouted.

Parked behind the airplane hangar was a very red, very fancy, very shiny Cadillac car. Its tires were new, and its hubcaps sparkled like diamonds.

"Get in, everyone!" Slick said. He hopped into the driver's seat and grabbed the fancy steering wheel.

Ashley and I jumped in the back seat. Clue tried to sit on Nick's lap, but I pulled her back. "No, Clue. You ride with us," I told her. Clue whined.

"Why *does* she like Nick so much?" Ashley whispered to me.

I shrugged. Slick started the car.

Vrrooomm!

We were off!

The Cadillac sped down the street. Rick reached over and found Christmas carols playing on the radio. We all sang along.

"This is fun," Ashley told me. "Except that singing Christmas carols reminds me of how little time we have left."

"I know. Christmas is only a few hours away," I said. "And Santa—I mean, S.C. has to land his plane at E.L.F. to pick up his special delivery. Or else no one will get their presents on time!"

We drove down Main Street. Christmas lights and decorations hung everywhere. Crowds of people rushed about, finishing their Christmas shopping. Everyone looked so happy. The grown-ups greeted each other with hugs and extra-wide smiles. The kids were bright-eyed with excitement.

"Don't you just love Christmas?" I cried.

Slick suddenly slammed on the car brakes. The car came to a screeching stop.

"What's happening? Are we there?" Ashley asked.

"No. But look." Slick pointed to a toy store a couple of feet away. A little boy and his mother gazed into the store window. The little boy was crying.

"Shhh," Slick said. "We should listen and find out why he's crying. It's sort of our job."

The storekeeper poked his head out the door. "Is anything wrong, Mrs. Johnson?" he called.

Mrs. Johnson shook her head. "We're fine, thank you." Mrs. Johnson put her arm around her little boy. "I'm sorry, Scotty," she quietly told him. "It costs too much."

"But I really want that space station set," Scotty cried. "I've been good this year."

Scotty's mom knelt down beside him. "I know you've been good," she said. "You've even been *extra* good. Maybe we can get the space station next year."

Nick began to cry.

"Nick, what's wrong?" I asked.

Nick pointed at my backpack. He was crying too hard to speak.

I unzipped my backpack and pulled out the stack of papers that made up the "Naughty" list. I scanned the list.

"Here he is," I said. "Scotty Johnson. Naughty." Now I felt like crying.

"Well, he's definitely *not* going to get his space station," Ashley said. "He's not going to get anything."

"And don't look for any presents under our tree either," I reminded Ashley. "We're on that list, too!"

Nick was really sobbing now. So were Rick and Slick.

"This is terrible," Nick said. "That awful hacker!"

"He's going to ruin Christmas for everybody!" Rick exclaimed.

"How could anyone be so mean?" Slick asked.

I turned to my sister. "Ashley, we've solved some pretty tough mysteries," I said. "But we've never cracked any case as important as this. It's up to us to save Christmas!"

Chapter 8

"Almost there!" Slick shouted.

The shiny red car zipped around another corner. I checked out the street sign. We were on Highbrow Lane.

Slick stopped the car. A huge six-story house towered over us.

"It's as big as a castle!" Nick exclaimed.

"Well, let's go inside," I said. "We have a hacker to catch!"

Nick, Rick, and Slick tumbled out of the car. Ashley and I followed. Clue ran after all of us. We hurried up to the house.

The front door of the house was about three times taller than us.

"Who can reach the doorbell?" I asked.

We stared helplessly at each other. None

of us was tall enough to reach it.

"Knock as hard as you can," I said. We all began to pound on the door.

The door suddenly flew open. I stumbled and fell into the entrance hall—and stared at the biggest pair of gleaming black shoes I had ever seen. I raised my eyes.

Looking down at me were a pair of curious brown eyes. They belonged to a very tall man. He was neatly dressed in a black suit and a crisp white shirt.

"May I help you?" His voice seemed to echo high above me.

I scrambled to my feet. "Uh—are you Roger E. Bencozees the Third?" I asked.

"I am not. I am Belmont, the butler," the man answered.

Ashley stepped forward. "Well, Belmont the butler, could you take us to see Roger E. Bencozees the Third?" she asked.

Belmont took off his glasses. He wiped them with his handkerchief. "I've never heard that name before," he said.

"You mean he doesn't live here?" Ashley asked.

"Sorry," Belmont replied. He pushed us toward the door.

"Wait!" I said. "We know for a fact that Roger lives here."

"How do you know that?" Nick whispered in my ear. "Is it some special detective's trick?"

I pointed to a pile of mail that was lying on the hall table. "It's no trick," I said. "That mail is addressed to Roger E. Bencozees the Third. So this must be his house."

Nick stepped up to Belmont. "Where is he?" he demanded.

"I'm sorry," Belmont answered. "But I have strict orders not to let Master Roger be disturbed."

Belmont spread out his arms and legs to block the doorway. Nick dove between Belmont's legs.

Belmont whirled around and grabbed Nick. He shook Nick's arm.

Grrrrrr. Woof!

Clue leaped at Belmont's ankles. She jumped up again and again, barking and barking.

"Get that wild animal away from me!" Belmont cried in a frightened voice.

"No way! Good girl, Clue! You keep him there," I shouted. "Let's go, everyone."

Ashley and I raced toward the stairs. Nick, Rick, and Slick were right behind us.

Clue stayed in the hall, yapping at Belmont. The huge butler was afraid to move.

We raced up the first few steps. The stairway was extra steep. It seemed to rise up forever.

"I'm going to find an elevator," Slick declared, turning back. "I hate climbing stairs."

"Stop! Stop, I say!" Belmont began chasing

us. He had gotten away from Clue.

"Sorry, Slick! Looks like you have to come with us," I shouted.

We raced up the rest of the stairs to the second floor. The hallway was lined with dozens of doors. They all looked exactly the same.

"Open every door," I yelled.

We raced down the hall. We opened each door and checked inside. There was no sign of Roger. We came to the end of the hallway.

"There's nothing here but another staircase," Nick cried in dismay.

I heard footsteps clomping behind us. And barking. Belmont appeared at the end of the hall. Clue was right behind him. She still nipped at his heels.

"Quick! Let's try the next floor," I said.

We raced up the stairs to the third floor. There were just as many doors, and no sign of Roger behind any of them.

We tried the fourth floor…the fifth

floor…and finally the sixth floor. We made it all the way down the hallway.

"This is it," I said. I paused to catch my breath. "This is the last door. Our last hope."

I stopped and took a deep breath—and flung open the door.

"Who are you? How did you get in here?" a boy about twelve years old asked. He sat at a desk in front of a fancy computer. His brown hair was neatly combed. He wore a white shirt and a dark vest.

Toys were stacked up around him on the desk. More toys spilled onto the floor. Even more toys were stuffed onto bookshelves and into drawers and closets.

Ashley and I looked at each other in surprise. Nick, Rick, and Slick stared in disbelief. None of us had ever seen one kid with so many toys!

"Are *you* Roger E. Bencozees?" I asked. "Are you the computer hacker?"

"What if I am?" Roger asked with a smirk.

"Why did you break into the E.L.F. Airlines computer?" Nick asked.

"Why did you try to keep the *Spirit of Christmas* from picking up its special delivery?" Rick asked.

"And why did you change the 'Nice' list so your name was the only one on it?" Slick asked.

"Are you kidding?" Roger asked. "So I could have more toys, that's why!" He turned toward the door.

"Belmont! Belmont, get in here!" Roger screamed. His face turned bright red.

Belmont raced into the room. He looked really tired. Sweat dripped down his face. He took big gulps of air.

"I thought I told you not to let anyone in here," Roger yelled. He stomped his feet angrily.

"I tried to keep them away," Belmont managed to say. "But this wild dog was chasing after me."

Clue dragged herself into the room and plopped down on the floor. She was also breathing hard.

"Some wild dog!" I laughed.

"She is wild. And she's mean," Belmont said.

"Clue isn't mean," Ashley told him.

"Not at all. *You're* the one who's mean," I said.

"If you were nice to Clue, she'd be nice to you," Ashley added.

"It's true. Why don't you pet her?" I said.

"Don't be nervous," Ashley told him. "Dogs can tell if you're nervous."

Belmont took a deep breath. Then he stuck his hand out toward Clue. Clue sniffed Belmont's fingers. Then she licked his hand.

Belmont smiled. "I think she likes me!" he said.

"Sure, Clue likes everyone," I told him. "And it's nice to be liked."

"It sure is!" Belmont said.

Roger scowled. "Well, I'm never nice to anyone," he snapped. "I hate everyone who's nice, and I hate everything that's nice. Especially Christmas! But Christmas won't be nice anymore. I fixed that!"

Nick, Rick, and Slick gasped in horror.

"How could anyone hate Christmas?" Nick asked.

"Why not? It's a stupid holiday," Roger went on. "*Anyone* can get presents at Christmas. Even silly, stupid people. Besides, I want to be the only one who gets presents."

Slick shook his fist at Roger. "Who are you calling stupid?" he yelled.

Nick and Rick grabbed Slick and held him back. They patted his shoulder to calm him down.

"You're making a mistake," I told Roger. "Breaking into other people's computers is dangerous—and it's against the law. You could get in big trouble."

"Plus it's very naughty," Nick added.

"Check your list! I'm the only one who *hasn't* been naughty this year," Roger boasted. He gave us a nasty smile.

"You changed the list. And now you have to change it back," Nick told him.

"And make the computer at E.L.F. work again," Rick added.

"Sorry, I can't help you," Roger said. "Belmont, show these people to the door. I have work to do. And toys to play with. Lots of them!"

Belmont frowned. "Yes, Master Roger." He opened the bedroom door and shooed us out.

"Good-bye," Roger called out after us. "Oh, and merry Christmas!" he shouted.

The door slammed shut. We could hear Roger inside, laughing.

"I'm sorry," Belmont told us. "No one ever tells Master Roger what to do."

"Until now," I said. "I have an idea."

I whispered my idea to Belmont, Ashley,

Nick, Rick, and Slick.

"Yes!" Ashley said.

Nick, Rick, and Slick slapped me a high five.

"That just might work," Belmont said.

Belmont pushed open Roger's door. We burst back into his bedroom.

"What are you doing? Belmont, throw those people out of here," Roger screamed and stamped his foot.

"I'm afraid I can't," Belmont replied. He began gathering Roger's toys together. "I'm taking these toys and giving them to all the children who really need them," he said.

"You can't do that!" Roger said. He stamped his foot again.

"Why not?" Belmont asked. "You're going to get hundreds of new toys tomorrow morning. And when you do, you won't even know these are gone."

Belmont reached for another toy. Roger grabbed it away from him.

"You can't take my toys! They're mine! All mine! I need them to play with!" Roger screamed.

"I don't think you really mean that," I told him.

"Why not?" Roger asked.

"Because there are an awful lot of kids all over the world," I began.

"And those kids are going to be really upset tomorrow morning when they don't get any Christmas presents," Ashley finished.

"So what?" Roger said.

"So all those kids are going to go after the one person who kept them from getting their presents. You!" I told him.

"That's right," Nick said. "Mary-Kate and Ashley are going to use their computers to send messages all over the world. They're going to tell kids everywhere that *you* ruined their Christmas!"

"Hundreds...thousands...millions of kids will rush right to your house!" Rick told him. "And they *won't* be very happy."

"Do you know what they'll do to you?" Slick asked.

We all waited to hear what Roger had to say.

"I don't care," Roger said. "I *still* want all the toys for myself."

Nick, Rick, and Slick sighed.

"You just don't understand, do you?" Nick asked. "Christmas isn't just about getting presents," he said.

"It's about *giving* presents, too," Rick added.

"About caring and understanding. About love and sharing," Slick said.

Roger laughed.

Nick, Rick, and Slick sadly shook their heads.

"Come on, guys," Ashley said. "We're wasting our time here."

We headed for the door. "Good-bye, Roger," I called back to him.

"Have a merry Christmas," Ashley added.

"If you *can* be merry, all by yourself," I said.

We started into the hall.

"Wait—what's that strange noise?" Belmont asked.

Chapter 10

"It sounds like someone crying," I said. "Could it be?"

We rushed back to Roger's room and pushed open the door. Roger was sitting on his bed, sobbing.

He saw us and tried to wipe the tears from his eyes. I sat down next to him. Clue licked his hand.

"What's wrong, Roger?" I asked. "You have all the toys you could want. And a huge room where you can play with them."

"And you have a great big computer," Nick said.

"You even have your very own butler," Slick added.

Roger lowered his head. "You're right. I

have everything. Everything—except friends." He cried even harder.

"I'm just like Ebenezer Scrooge," Roger went on. "I tried to ruin everyone's Christmas. Now everyone will really hate me. I'll be lonely—forever! Just like Ebenezer Scrooge."

"There's still time to fix that," I told him. "The original Scrooge learned a lot about the joy of sharing with others. Then he wasn't lonely anymore."

"But first we need to find the *Spirit of Christmas*," Ashley said. "And to do that we need to get the E.L.F. Airlines computer running again," she added.

"I can do that right now!" Roger jumped up and ran to his computer. He began typing commands on his keyboard.

"There. I fixed it. Your computer is working again," he told Nick, Rick, and Slick.

"Hooray!" Nick, Rick, and Slick cheered.

"You're okay, Roger!" Ashley told him.

Belmont hugged Roger tight.

"What are we waiting for?" Nick shouted. "Let's get back to E.L.F. and bring in our plane!"

"Wait!" Roger shouted. "Can…can I come with you?" he asked.

"Sure," I said. "We can use your help."

Roger turned to Nick, Rick, and Slick. "I'm sorry for what I did," he told them. "Will you be my friends?"

"Absolutely," Nick shouted.

"Positively," Rick agreed.

"Double definitely," Slick added. "Now let's go!"

We all raced down the long staircase and out the front door. We piled into the shiny red Cadillac, and Slick quickly drove us back to E.L.F.

In no time at all, the BIG computer found the *Spirit of Christmas*.

"Roger, you type the landing instructions into the BIG computer," Nick told him. "The

BIG computer will send the instructions to the plane's computer on the *Spirit of Christmas*. The plane will practically land itself!"

Roger did it, and a few minutes later we heard an airplane overhead. We rushed outside. The *Spirit of Christmas* touched down onto the runway. Its wheels screeched to a stop.

"The boss is coming," Nick called.

"We need to get ready," Rick said.

"Oh, my, we'd better hurry. We can't let the boss see that we're out of our real uniforms!" Slick added.

Nick, Rick, and Slick spun around. A puff of smoke suddenly filled the air.

"What's happening to them?" Roger asked.

"I don't know. It's like some kind of magic," I answered.

The smoke cleared.

Nick, Rick, and Slick stood in front of us. Their blue overalls were gone. They wore bright red shirts and little green hats. Green tights covered their legs. On their feet were pointed green shoes.

"Are those your real uniforms?" I asked.

"That's right," Nick told me.

"We're elves!" Rick and Slick shouted. "Santa's helpers!"

"Are you surprised?" Slick asked Ashley and me.

"Not really," I answered. "Don't forget, Ashley and I *are* detectives."

"It was only logical," Ashley added.

The plane door swung open wide. A pair of shiny black boots appeared. Then a bright red suit, an enormous belly, and a long, fluffy white beard.

Ashley and I stared. Ashley leaned over and whispered in my ear. "Mary-Kate, it *is* really him, isn't it?" she asked.

"Definitely," I told her.

Roger's mouth dropped open in astonishment. "That—that's Santa!" he said. "Wow!"

"Merry Christmas!" Santa called to us all. "Ho! Ho! Ho!"

"Merry Christmas!" Ashley and I replied.

Nick, Rick, and Slick turned and ran into the airplane hangar. They came back pushing carts piled high with presents of every weight, shape, and size. They loaded them into the *Spirit of Christmas*.

"Wait right here!" Nick said. He and Rick ran into the control room. Seconds later they returned with armfuls of computer printouts. They handed them to Santa.

"Here's your *new* flight schedule," Nick said. "And the latest weather reports—from the Rocky Mountains to the Great Wall of China and beyond!"

"But most important, here are the *real* 'Naughty' and 'Nice' lists!" Rick said.

This time the "Nice" list was a lot bigger than the "Naughty" list. A *lot* bigger!

Santa beamed with pleasure. "The really BIG computer just made my job a lot easier.

I might even decide to visit everyone *twice* a year," he joked. "Ho! Ho! Ho! You all did a really great job!"

"Well, we did have a little trouble at first," Nick told him. "But Mary-Kate and Ashley saved the day," he added.

"Of course," Santa said. "The Trenchcoat Twins will solve any crime. In this case—by Christmas time!"

Santa winked at Ashley and me. "Now, is there something I can do to thank you for saving the *Spirit of Christmas*?" he asked.

Ashley and I whispered to each other. "Well, there is one little thing," I began.

"Could you please take our names off the 'Naughty' list?" Ashley asked.

"And Trent and Lizzie, too," I added.

Santa roared with laughter. "You're already off the list! You weren't even close to being naughty," he told us.

Roger's face flushed bright red. Santa stared at him. Then he put his arm around

Roger's shoulders.

"Don't worry, Roger," he said. "I have a very short memory!" Santa winked at Roger. "I'm just glad you learned the true meaning of Christmas," he said.

Nick looked at his watch. "Santa—you had better go! You have toys to deliver!"

We watched as Santa climbed back into the plane. The *Spirit of Christmas* took off. We waved until we couldn't see the plane anymore.

"Yikes! Ashley, we have to get going, too," I said.

We said good-bye to Nick, Rick, Slick, and Roger and hopped on our bikes. "Come on, Clue!" I called.

Clue ran up to Nick. She licked at his hands. She whined and wagged her tail.

"No wonder Clue likes you so much," I told Nick. "I guess she knew you were an elf all along."

"It's not just that," Nick said. He reached

into his pocket. "It's also because I carry these around!"

Nick opened his hand. "Dog yummies!" he said. Clue gulped down the treats, and Nick patted her on the head one last time.

I lifted Clue into the basket on my bike. Ashley and I headed toward home.

"Another case solved," I said.

"I don't want to upset you," Ashley said. "But you're forgetting one thing. We have one more mystery to solve."

"What mystery?" I asked.

"How to explain to Mom and Dad why we *didn't* clean up the mess in the attic!" Ashley answered.

Chapter  11

We parked our bikes in the driveway and raced up the back stairs. We climbed up to the attic. We were almost at our office door when Mom's voice called out.

"Hey, you two. Where have you been?"

Mom waited at the bottom of the stairs. "I've been looking all over for you," she said. "I need you to help me wrap some presents after dinner." She smiled at us.

"Uh…sure, Mom," I said.

"We'd love to help," Ashley added.

"Good." Mom walked away. "Better wash up soon. Dinner's almost ready," she said.

"Why didn't she yell at us about the mess in the attic?" I whispered to Ashley.

Ashley shrugged.

I opened the attic door and flicked on the lights. "What happened?" I exclaimed.

The room was spotless! The broken ornaments were all cleaned up. Our detective supplies were neatly stacked back on the shelves. The Christmas tree stood tall with all the decorations in place and the lights shining brightly.

Trent was hanging a last piece of tinsel on the tree.

My mouth dropped open in surprise. "Trent? You did all this?" I asked.

"I can't believe it!" Ashley exclaimed.

Trent shrugged. "Well, it *is* Christmas Eve and—"

"And you didn't want to be naughty, right?" I teased him.

"No," Trent said with a puzzled expression. "It was kind of weird. This strange feeling came over me. I guess it was Christmas spirit. I just felt like doing something good."

"Really?" I asked. Ashley and I stared at

Trent in disbelief.

"Really. Or maybe I wanted to make sure I got some great presents tomorrow morning," Trent said. He burst out laughing and hurried out of the room.

"Tell me something, Mary-Kate," Ashley said. "Did Trent really do something nice for us? Did he really get some Christmas spirit?"

"I don't know, Ashley," I answered. "I guess that's one mystery we're never going to solve!"

Hi — from both of us!

Ho! Ho! Ho! That's what Ashley and I said when we caught the naughty boy who tried to ruin Christmas! Lucky for us, we figured out how to use our computers to crack that case. But computers couldn't help solve our *next* big mystery.

We were headed back to Sea World® to investigate three daring pirates and some amazing *singing* sharks. Singing sharks? There are no such things as singing sharks—or are there? We had to find out fast. The whole future of Sea World® depended on us!

Read all about it in *The Case Of The Shark Encounter*. And, in the meantime, if you have any questions, you can write us at:

MARY-KATE + ASHLEY'S FUN CLUB™
859 HOLLYWOOD WAY, SUITE 412
BURBANK, CA 91505

We would love to hear from you!

Love
Mary-Kate and Ashley

A brand-new book series starring the Olsen Twins!
Based on their best-selling detective home video series.

Join the Trenchcoat Twins™—Mary-Kate and Ashley—as
they find mystery, adventure, and fun!

Book One:
The Case Of The Sea World® Adventure™
Book Two:
The Case Of The Mystery Cruise™
Book Three:
The Case Of The Fun House Mystery™
Book Four:
The Case Of The U.S. Space Camp® Mission™
Book Five:
The Case Of The Christmas Caper™
Book Six:
The Case Of The Shark Encounter™
(coming February 1997)
And Super Special #1:
from their other best-selling home video series
You're Invited To Mary-Kate & Ashley's™
Sleepover Party™
A book with a special Mary-Kate & Ashley locket
just for you!
**Look for these great books all year long from Dualstar Publications and
Parachute Press, Inc., published by *Scholastic*.**

TM & © 1996 Dualstar Entertainment Group, Inc.

HOLLYWOOD
SWEEPSTAKES

YOU CAN WIN A TRIP TO HOLLYWOOD TO MEET MARY-KATE & ASHLEY!

Complete this entry form and send to:

The Adventures of Mary-Kate & Ashley™ Hollywood Sweepstakes
c/o Scholastic Trade Marketing Dept.
P.O. Box 7500
Jefferson City, MO 65102-7500

MARY-KATE & ASHLEY SWEEPSTAKES

Name_____ *(please print)* _____

Address_____

City_____ State_____ Zip_____

Phone Number (_____) _____

Age_____

DUALSTAR
PUBLICATIONS

No purchase necessary to enter.
Sweepstakes entries must be received by 4/15/97.

The Adventures of Mary-Kate & Ashley™ Hollywood Sweepstakes

OFFICIAL RULES:

1. No purchase necessary.

2. To enter, complete this official entry form or hand print your name, address, day and evening phone numbers along with the words "The Adventures of Mary-Kate & Ashley™ Hollywood Sweepstakes" on a 3" X 5" card and mail to The Adventures of Mary-Kate & Ashley™ Hollywood Sweepstakes, c/o Scholastic Trade Marketing Dept., P.O. Box 7500, Jefferson City, MO 65102-7500. Enter as often as you wish, but each entry must be mailed separately. One entry per envelope. Partially completed, illegible or mechanically reproduced entries will not be accepted. All entries must be received no later than April 15, 1997. Sponsors not responsible for delayed, damaged, lost, late, misdirected, incomplete, postage due mail, or illegible entries. All entries become the property of Scholastic, Inc. and will not be returned.

3. Sweepstakes open to U.S. residents who are between the ages of five and twelve years old by April 30, 1997, excluding employees of Scholastic Inc., Parachute Press, Inc., Warner Vision Entertainment Inc., Dualstar Entertainment Group, Inc., and their respective parent companies, affiliates, subsidiaries, advertising, promotion and fulfillment agencies, and the persons with whom each of the above are domiciled. Sweepstakes is void where prohibited by law.

4. One (1) Grand Prize winner will receive a Hollywood Weekend Adventure for a family of four to Hollywood, California. Trip includes: round trip coach airfare from airport nearest winner's home to Los Angeles airport; hotel accommodations for two (2) nights (1 double room); mid-sized rental car (eligible drivers only); $500 spending money, and ice cream party with Mary-Kate & Ashley Olsen. (Estimated retail value $3000). Grand Prize winners must utilize prize within one year from day of notification. Travel must include Saturday night stay. Date of trip to be decided by Dualstar Entertainment Group, Inc.

5. Odds of winning depend on total number of entries received. All prizes will be awarded. Winners will be selected in a random drawing on or about April 30, 1997, by Scholastic Inc., whose decisions are final. Winners will be notified by mail. Winners will be required to complete an affidavit of eligibility. Grand Prize winners and their guests must sign and return a liability and publicity release within 14 days of receipt. By acceptance of their prize, winners consent to the use of their names and photographs or likenesses by Scholastic Inc., Parachute Press, Inc., Dualstar Entertainment Group, Inc. and for publicity purposes without further compensation except where prohibited.

6. Only one prize will be awarded per individual, family, or household. Prizes are non-transferable, non-returnable, and cannot be sold or redeemed for cash. No substitutions allowed. Any federal, state, and local taxes on prizes are the sole responsibility of the winner. All federal, state, and local laws apply.

7. For a list of winners or a complete set of rules, send a self-addressed stamped envelope (excluding residents of Vermont and Washington) after April 30, 1997 to The Adventures of Mary-Kate & Ashley™ Hollywood Sweepstakes Winners List, c/o Scholastic Trade Marketing Dept., P.O. Box 7500, Jefferson City, MO 65102-7500.

TM & © 1997 Dualstar Entertainment Group, Inc., Dualstar Video and all logos, character names, and other likenesses thereof are the trademarks of Dualstar Entertainment Group, Inc. All rights reserved.

The Adventures of
MARY-KATE & ASHLEY™

Look for the best-selling detective home video episodes.

The Case Of The Volcano Adventure™	**Spring 97 Release**
The Case Of The U.S. Navy Mystery™	**Spring 97 Release**
The Case Of The Hotel Who•Done•It™ *NEW*	53328-3
The Case Of The Shark Encounter™	53320-3
The Case Of The U.S. Space Camp® Mission™	53321-3
The Case Of The Fun House Mystery™	53306-3
The Case Of The Christmas Caper™	53305-3
The Case Of The Sea World® Adventure™	53301-3
The Case Of The Mystery Cruise™	53302-3
The Case Of The Logical i Ranch™	53303-3
The Case Of Thorn Mansion™	53300-3

Join the fun!

You're Invited To Mary-Kate & Ashley's™ Sleepover Party™	53307-3
You're Invited To Mary-Kate & Ashley's™ Hawaiian Beach Party™ *NEW*	53329-3

And also available:

Mary-Kate and Ashley Olsen: Our First Video™	53304-3

DUALSTAR VIDEO

Distributed by KidVision, a division of Warner Vision Entertainment. All rights reserved.
A Warner Music Group Company.
TM & ©1996 Dualstar Entertainment Group, Inc.

It doesn't matter if you live around the corner...
or around the world...
If you are a fan of Mary-Kate and Ashley Olsen,
you should be a member of

MARY-KATE + ASHLEY'S FUN CLUB™

Here's what you get:
Our Funzine™
An autographed color photo
Two black & white individual photos
A full size color poster
An official **Fun Club**™ membership card
A **Fun Club**™ school folder
Two special **Fun Club**™ surprises
A holiday card
Fun Club™ collectibles catalog
Plus a **Fun Club**™ box to keep everything in

To join Mary-Kate + Ashley's Fun Club™, fill out the form
below and send it along with

U.S. Residents – $17.00
Canadian Residents – $22 U.S. Funds
International Residents – $27 U.S. Funds

MARY-KATE + ASHLEY'S FUN CLUB™
859 HOLLYWOOD WAY, SUITE 275
BURBANK, CA 91505

NAME:_____

ADDRESS:_____

CITY:_____STATE:_____ZIP:_____

PHONE: (____) _____BIRTHDATE:_____

TM & © 1996 Dualstar Entertainment Group, Inc.

What's on the Top
of Your Holiday List?

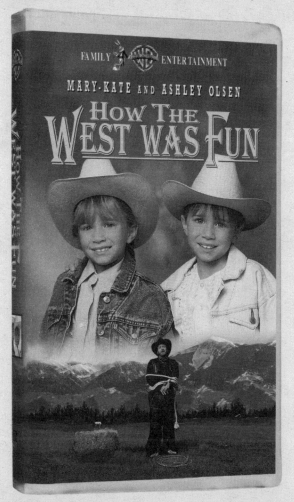

Own It On Video!

©1994 Dualstar Productions and Green/Epstein Productions, Inc. In Association with Warner Bros. Television.
©1996 Warner Home Video.